Christmas can't be jolly all the time.

CONTENTS

Anti-Claus

Anti-Claus

When December came, everything in the village changed. Once vibrant voices grew hushed and the tinkle of laughter fell away. Joy was forgotten. A blanket of fear descended, heavier even than the prodigious snowfall. People hurried through the streets, afraid to be out alone after dark.

He was coming.

Santa Claus.

Every year it was the same but the burden never got any easier. In the summer months, when the bright sunshine reigned supreme, there was always a little knot of fear in the villagers' stomachs, knowing that the reprieve was only temporary. Winter would soon come, and with it the iron grip of the cold and the infinite darkness.

With two weeks to go, final preparations began. All decorations and ornaments were taken down, boxed up and hidden in attics. The indoor trees, situated in the corners of every village house and nurtured throughout the year, were taken outside and left to fend for themselves until January broke. The favourite toys of all the children were put to one side of the chimneys and left untouched. So too were the items most prized by the adults.

When the time came, in the dark and early hours of the 25th of December, Santa Claus would crawl down their chimneys and take what he wanted.

Lily Tomlinson had been badly-behaved all year – bottom of the class in virtually every subject and always forgetting to do her homework. She'd not once helped her mother with the housework, despite being asked often. Her face was usually scrunched in a scowl and she was always climbing trees and coming home covered in muck. At least once a week she'd be involved in a fight, usually with one of the boys. She was getting a bit of a reputation.

When summer was almost over, her parents had bought her a puppy, in the hope of turning her into a good little girl. Quite how this was to be achieved they had no idea, but they nursed the forlorn hope that the tiny dog would bond with her and somehow bring out an angel that hadn't yet materialised.   There could be no doubt that Lily loved that puppy with all her heart, and that the feeling was wholly reciprocated, but having a new, constant companion didn't change her behaviour one bit.

Her parents despaired. They had, in their foolishness, given her the one thing that Santa Claus would certainly take, which would only make the following year even more unbearable.

But there was another fear, lurking in their bellies. Every year, the most badly-behaved of the villagers was lashed to death out on the village green, their skin flayed in great strips as Santa's reindeer-hide whip gouged deep crimson wounds and sent blood flying across the pristine, white snow. The others, even the children, would peer through the gaps in their curtains, cold sweats on their own skin, until the deed was over. Only when Santa Claus was gone would they come out and tend to the body, which would be buried at noon the next day. The name of the deceased would be added to the list of Terrible People, carved into the stone marker at the crossroads.

There could be no greater disgrace.

Her parents hoped that this year, it wouldn't be Lily out there.

On the 25th of December, in the early hours of the morning, a clatter reverberated through the house as something large forced its way down the chimney and into the Tomlinson's lounge. Awake, too frightened to move, Lily's parents cowered under their blanket and listened, their ears straining. They heard Santa Claus rummaging through their belongings, and a short, deep growl of appreciation when he found something he wanted.

And then came the sound of his footsteps on the stairs.

Clump-clump-clump.

Heavy footsteps, a grunt accompanying each one.

In her bedroom, Lily was awakened by growling. Pongo was standing at the end of their bed, his hackles raised, staring and snarling at the door. Lily sat up and listened. Footsteps made their way along the landing.

He was outside.

The bedroom door opened. A bulky figure stood in the doorway, somehow blacker than the darkness around it. The dog let out a small whine and was silent. Lily felt her feet grow warm. Pongo, in his terror, had wet the bed.

Santa Claus stepped into the room. He waited, saying nothing, only the sound of his heavy breathing in the darkness.

"What do you want?" asked Lily, her voice barely more than a croak.

"The dog," said Santa. His voice was deep. Gravelly. Very, very old. "Give it to me."

Lily reached for the dog and pulled it under the duvet.

"Never!" she screamed.

The defiance was only temporary. Santa ripped away the duvet and flung it across the room. With a roar, he grabbed Pongo by the scruff of his neck and, with his other hand, delivered a blow that sent Lily flying from the bed and into the wall. There was a sickening crunch as her neck broke and she lay there, quite dead.

With Pongo whining in terror, Santa clumped his way out of the room and down the stairs. Outside, screams rang through the streets as one of the men-folk was dragged by his hair and tied to the village whipping post by half a dozen small figures dressed in black robes.

"Please!" he wailed. "I haven't done anything wrong!"

"Ho ho ho!" laughed Santa, his deep voice echoing around the village square. "Hasn't done anything wrong! Listen to him!"

With a quick flick of his wrist, he snapped the dog's neck and threw the body into his sack. People were staring through their windows, watching the scene unfold. Some of the braver souls had come out onto the square.

"Let him go!" shouted a woman, but her defiance was fleeting as she fled when Santa turned his gaze on her.

"Listen to me!" he boomed, reaching for his whip. "Thomas Kelp is the worst of all of you, and that is saying something. You people just can't be good, can you? Even though you know I come to punish you, every year without fail, you still think you can get away with whatever you like."

He rolled up his sleeves and tested the whip. The tip broke through the snow and smashed against the cobbled stones, sending a loud *crack!* through the streets.

"What has he done?" asked another voice.

Santa laughed again. "I'll tell you," he roared. "He stole a loaf of bread from his employer. He hit his wife and made her bleed. He lied, just now, about not doing anything wrong. But worse than any of this," he said, turning his gaze on the owner of the enquiring voice before looking down at Thomas Kelp, "he told his only child that I did not exist!"

"I didn't want to scare him," pleaded Kelp, his eyes wide. "I didn't want him growing up in fear like the rest of us."

"QUIET!" shouted Santa. He lifted up his arm and brought the whip down across Thomas Kelp's back. It cut through his shirt and left a ragged tear in the man's flesh. Kelp moaned in terror and pain and Santa brought the whip down again and again until Kelp was silenced.

As the villagers watched, Santa kept whipping until the flesh was lashed from Kelp's bones. The whip came away soaked in blood, flinging great dollops of fatty flesh onto the snow at the villagers' feet. The punishment continued long after Kelp was dead, until the man was no longer recognisable as having once been a living person.

When it was over, Santa held out the whip and it was retrieved by one of his little helpers. He turned to look at the villagers one last time.

"I will see you all again, one year from now," he said, bowing his head. And then he left, walking into the darkness surrounded by his little helpers, off to where they had parked up the sled. In moments, they were flying through the air to the next village.

It was a long night.

Elf Abuse

Elf Abuse

When the 1st of December came around and Santa inspected the productivity against the scheduled quotas, he realised that there was quite a considerable deficit. His cheeks reddened with anger and behind his bushy white beard he gnashed his teeth. He stormed into the workshop, shaking his fat fist at the assembled elves.

"You little shits!" he screamed. "What the fuck have you been doing all year? Have you SEEN how behind we are?"

The elves flinched at the harshness of Santa's voice, even though they were used to this sort of thing. Every year, it was always the same. They worked harder than ever, for very little thanks, and each year they managed to pull off the impossible. Every good child out there always got what they wanted on Christmas Day.

Dauphin put his little hand in the air.

"What is it?" snapped Santa.

"We need more elves!" he said in a squeaky voice.

"MORE ELVES?" roared Santa, livid with rage. "You little bastards need to work harder, that's all there is to it! You're getting lazier and lazier. Don't make me fetch the whip again! Get it sorted!"

With that, Santa turned and stormed back out of the workshop. The elves sat around in silence for a while, looking at each other with wide eyes. They remembered the last time Santa got his whip out. Three elves died and Rango still walked with a limp.

"Big fat prick," said Dauphin, causing a few of the others to giggle nervously.

"What are we going to do?" asked one.

"You'll see," said Dauphin, winking. "I have a plan. Somebody pass me a phone."

The next morning, three government inspectors arrived at the North Pole. They were directed to Santa's Grotto by a friendly polar bear.

Santa was flopped out on a huge leather sofa, a half empty bottle of whisky on the floor next to him.

"Who the fuck are you?" he asked.

The men walked over and stood on a reindeer-skin rug, the head still attached. It had a red nose and a startled expression. Rudolph had met a rather undignified end a few years previously when a drunk Santa had axed him to death for rejecting his sexual advances.

"We're from the Department of Social Services," said one of the men, offering his hand.

Santa ignored the gesture.

"Well, what the fuck do you want?" he asked.

"We've had a complaint of elf abuse," said the man. "We've come to investigate."

Santa sat up straight on the sofa and glared at them.

"No need to investigate," he said at last. "I'll admit it right now. The little cunts need a good slapping every now and then, and there's no-one else around here that can do it."

"You are aware that there's a statute against harming an elf?" said the man as the others looked on impassively. "Nobody can ignore it, not even you."

"Then tell me this," said Santa, stepping forward and jabbing a finger aggressively at the man's chest. "If I don't knock these pricks into shape, the toys don't get made. And if the toys don't get made, there's going to be millions of disappointed children on Christmas Day. Is that what you want?"

"Of course not."

"Well, what's the answer?"

"More elves?"

Santa hooted with laughter, but it was a nasty sort of laughter with an undercurrent of bitterness.

"I asked for a bigger budget for more elves two years ago and you bastards turned me down flat."

"I understand your position, Mr Claus, but-"

"NO YOU FUCKING DON'T!" roared Santa, throwing his hands in the air in exasperation. He paced the room, ranting. "You come here and ask the impossible! You can't have it both ways – tell me, do you want the toy quota to be met or do you want these little shits to fail? One or the other, which is it?"

"All I know," said the man, "is that the elf abuse has to stop."

"Very well," said Santa, smiling hatefully. "Just remember you said that."

On Christmas Day, eight year old Sally Hopkins woke up and rushed downstairs to the Christmas tree to see what Santa had left there for her. She'd been a very good girl all year and the one thing she wanted more than anything else was a Kim Kardashian doll, the one with the big fat ass. But the space beneath the tree was empty.

There were no presents.

She started to cry, and then started to wail, so much so that her parents woke up and came rushing down the stairs to see what was wrong.

"No presents!" cried Sally, distraught.

Her parents looked at each other, confused.

It was the same story up and down the land. Good children were waking up to a complete lack of presents and Christmas Day was ruined for thousands of families. Thousands of letters of complaint were written and sent to the North Pole. Santa read them all and roared with laughter. When he finally managed to contain his mirth, he put them all in a big red sack and went out in the sled to drop them off at the local government offices.

Two days later, a delegation of big cheeses turned up at Santa's grotto.

"I fucking told you!" shouted Santa, his beard soaked with rage-foam. "This is what you wanted!"

One of the government heads stepped forwards, his face grim.

"We hear you, Mr Claus," he said. "And this cannot happen again. Come what may, the good children must get their presents."

"So I have free reign to ensure the productivity levels are met?" asked Santa.

"The statute regarding elf harm has been rescinded," said the man.

"That's more like it. Now, is that all?"

"I think so."

"Good. Now fuck off."

When December the 1st finally came around again, Santa inspected the productivity against the scheduled quotas and saw that there was, once more, quite a considerable deficit.

Calmly, he went to fetch his whip.

He was smiling.

The
Christmas
Party

The Christmas Party

Nurse Hammond woke up feeling sore all over and hoped she wasn't getting a virus. That would be the last thing she needed. The residents were bad enough without the hassle of being ill. There was already the additional excitement of the Christmas and New Year period - God only knows what they'd get up to if she wasn't on top of her game.

Some may think Nurse Hammond was an especially strict disciplinarian, heavy-handed in her management of the residents of the Sunnyville Care Home, but such judgement could only come from these do-good sorts that didn't have to deal with these animals on a daily basis. Truth be told, putting a bunch of old people together under one roof was a recipe for disaster. The ones that could still think properly were always up to no good – smuggling booze in one week, running gambling dens the next. And they were always at it. *Sex*. The thought of it made her sick.

She was in a particularly foul mood because the previous day was Christmas Day and the evening's party had gotten somewhat out of control. There was a list of transgressions as long as her arm. She knew it was a mistake to allow them the privilege of enjoying themselves.

Before the pressure of it all had become too much to bear, and she had somehow made her way to bed, she remembered finding a stash of alcopops in the broom cupboard. A more thorough search had revealed some cellophane-wrapped marijuana hidden in one of the cisterns. *Marijuana!* And all this before she had to turn away the strippers. Honestly, not one of the residents was under seventy-five years of age and here they were, acting like Godless teenagers! She should never have tried to police the party on her own, but running the home meant keeping a tight control of the budget and there was no way she could afford to pay the other carers double-time, especially when they'd be on it for all of Boxing Day as well.

No, it wouldn't do. As soon as the early morning shift clocked on, Nurse Hammond ordered them to gather together all of the residents in the dining hall at 9am prompt.

Preceding this, she went about her rounds. Her head was pounding and all she really wanted to do was go back to bed. The residents were all staggering about, even more decrepit than usual, no doubt nursing hangovers. Well, it was all they deserved. One or two caught her eye and turned away smirking, no doubt thinking they'd gotten away with it. Wally Pitkin, the scrawny little troublemaker, gave her a particularly ugly leer, the sight of his black teeth threatening to make her vomit. Edna Gittings, a right nasty piece of work, was right there next to him, whispering in his ear, something that made them both laugh out loud. What a shock they'd be getting!

She checked all of the rooms, relishing the thought of delivering the mother of all bollockings. They wouldn't know what had hit them. There would be no puddings until after the New Year. No television in the main sitting room. Board games would be locked away (including jigsaws). No gatherings of more than two residents at a time. Small punishments but cumulative, enough to make their lives even more miserable than usual. They had to learn.

At 9am prompt, Nurse Hammond strode into the dining area and stood looking at them all for a few seconds. Ever professional, she always managed to tamp down the hatred in her voice, and she used this brief time to compose herself. They looked back at her, eyes twinkling, even now trying to hide their smirks.

"We all know why I've called this meeting," she announced at last. "This disgraceful behaviour has no place at Sunnyville. We have a reputation to uphold."

Wally Pitkin let out a loud hoot of laughter.

"Something to say, Mr Pitkin?" she snapped.

He shook his head and settled back down.

"I thought not. Disgusting, the lot of you! Well, last night was the final straw. There will be no more Christmas parties. And nobody will be staying up to see in the New Year – lights out will be at nine o'clock and anybody caught out of their room will be taken down to the medical room and sedated. Do you hear me?"

This time, it was Edna Gittings who let out a shrill hoot of laughter. The sound made Nurse Hammond wince, cutting right through her skull and aggravating her pounding headache. She ignored the sound and proceeded to list their misdemeanours from the previous night. As she talked, she couldn't help but notice the crowd getting agitated, stirring with uncharacteristic energy, unable to stifle the odd guffaw.

"Really!" she snapped, getting angry. "What is wrong with you people this morning?"

"How's your head?" said Willy Pitkin, causing a ripple of laughter.

"My head? What business is that of yours?"

"You snaffled up enough of my bloody gin last night! I'm amazed you're even up and out of bed."

"Don't be ridiculous," she said.

"It's true!" shouted Lizzie Hindlip, cackling. "We all saw you!"

"I'm warning you," said Nurse Hammond, feeling her blood beginning to boil.

"You're warning us!" shouted Wally, almost collapsing with mirth. "That's funny. Really. At first we only spiked your drinks but after a point you couldn't get enough of the stuff! Don't you remember, Nurse Hammond?"

She tried to think back, to remember the latter stages of the previous night. She couldn't.

"Let me show you something that might change your mind about one or two things," said Wally.

There was something about the tone of his voice that made Nurse Hammond go cold inside. She watched as Wally stood and walked over to the wall mounted television set. He turned it on and popped a disc into the dvd player beneath it.

"This is just a copy, obviously," he said, grinning.

The screen filled with a video clip of Nurse Hammond, naked and clearly off her head, being fucked senseless by a Great Dane that had mounted her from behind. The residents were standing around, laughing and clapping.

"Oh, it was a corker of a night, Nurse Hammond," said Wally, his voice quiet. "Now, tell us again, what time will the New Year party be starting?"

Glitter

Glitter

I've been seeing it for years, ever since I was a boy. Dog shit sprinkled with glitter, out on the streets of my home town. I'd see it so often that I didn't even think it was unusual. Back when it was crumbly white, that's how long ago I'm talking, although you don't see it these days. But shit is always lying around, despite the fines handed out to owners who don't clear up after their pets. Some of them just don't seem to care.

It's not something I pay much attention to, the shit and the glitter, not really. I mean I see it, and sometimes muse on it, but not for long - it isn't something I think about in any great depth. You know that life sometimes has little mysteries that you just accept? Like the way birds sometimes fly into windows, or the way it can rain on one half of the street and not the other? It's like that.

Or rather it was. Because this morning, the mystery was solved. I saw him, this old man, stooping over to pour a little bit of glitter on a fresh turd. It stopped me in my tracks, the craziness of it. And for some reason I needed to know what this was all about. So I followed him.

He did it twice more before he suspected that he was being followed. I'm no sleuth and I wasn't very good at concealing myself. He turned and looked at me for a long time before moving on. At that point I could've walked away but I decided not to. I don't know why. It wasn't really any of my business but now that I'd seen it happening, rather than just seeing the aftermath, my curiosity was piqued. I kept following him, into town, even though this was going to make me late for work.

Eventually he stopped and waited for me to catch up.

"What are you looking at?" he asked.

"Nothing."

"Don't lie. You've been following me. I ain't stupid."

I'd been caught red-handed, there wasn't much point in denying it.

"OK," I said, "you got me. I'm curious, that's all. About the glitter."

"You want me to tell you why I put glitter on the dog shits?"

"Yes."

He looked me up and down and sighed.

"No-one's ever asked before," he said.

"Really? But you must have been doing it for over twenty years."

"More like sixty years, son. Ever since I was a boy." He looked around and pointed at a small café. "Why don't you buy us a hot drink and I'll tell you all about it."

The café was fairly dingy inside. I'd never been there before, never even noticed its existence. We were the only customers. I ordered a tea for the old man and a coffee for myself. The young girl behind the counter (who was very attractive, I noticed) told me to sit and she'd bring them over.

We sat by the window, looking out onto the street. The old man sat quietly, waiting for his drink, occasionally looking my way. He seemed unsure now, as though maybe he thought he'd made a mistake. The drinks arrived and we each took a sip.

"Do you like Christmas, boy?" he asked.

"Yeah. I mean, who doesn't?"

"Not everyone does. If you haven't got any loved ones, or any money, Christmas can be a hard time. The suicide rates go right up at Christmas, did you know that?"

"I think so, yeah."

"It's terrible really. Should be a time for celebration, not for death. You get lots of presents, do you?"

"I used to. Not so much now."

He smiled. "I never used to care much about presents," he said. "My family was dirt poor and I'd be grateful for a fresh orange on Christmas Day. Can you believe that?"

I didn't know what to say. I've never been grateful for a piece of fruit in my life. They're sort of everywhere. I'd have been heartbroken if my parents had fobbed me off with an orange.

"I don't suppose you can," he said, still smiling and looking at me until I had to break eye contact and feign interest in something outside the window. "Youngsters these days get everything they want. It's a different world from the one I grew up in."

I began to wonder where all of this was going. I was conscious of the bollocking I'd get for being late for work – it would be the second time in a week and my boss was only going to take so much. I got the feeling that this old man was a bit lonely and, grateful for company, could sit there talking for hours. As soon as that thought crossed my mind I felt guilty for wanting to get away and deprive him of some human contact.

"I'll tell you about the glitter," he said, as though sensing my thoughts. "Have you ever been to the North Pole?"

"Er, no."

"I have. I loved Christmas so much that I begged my parents to take me. They couldn't afford it, of course. But when some distant relative died and left my father some money, he took me. All those years of thanking him for the oranges must have eaten away at him and this was his was of making amends. We caught a flight up to Lapland on the twenty-second of December and did the whole tourist thing. At least that's what I thought it was – Santa and all his reindeer, all the elves rushing about with toys. Even as a child I knew this was all make-believe. Isn't that right, son?"

"Isn't what right?"

"That it's all make-believe? Some tour company dressing up their employees to make a bit of money from people's stupidity."

"I guess so."

"Wrong!" he said, adding a cackle for good measure. "It's all real! That man I saw really was Santa Claus! They really were elves. And the reindeer, the beautiful reindeer…. They were always my favourites. Rudolph, Dasher, Dancer, Prancer, Vixen, Comet, Cupid, Donner and Blitzen."

"You know all their names from memory?" I asked. "I can never remember more than a couple."

"They were my favourite part of Christmas," he said, his eyes turning misty with nostalgia. "More than the presents, more than the elves, more than Santa, even…. I loved the reindeer and spent most of my time in the North Pole petting them. They were magnificent beasts. Anyway, as things turned out, there was something wrong with the plane that was supposed to fly us home so we ended up staying another couple of days until they sorted it out. We saw Santa and his reindeer fly off on Christmas Eve to deliver the presents. And we were still there when they came back."

He trailed off and I noticed that his eyes were glazed over. A single tear rolled down his cheek.

"What happened?" I asked.

"The reindeer had aged terribly overnight. They were so exhausted from flying around the world, delivering all those presents, it had taken everything from them. One by one, as I watched in horror, the poor creatures dropped down dead in the snow. My father tried to drag me away but I ran over to Rudolph and flung myself across him. He was still warm. I stayed there until he turned cold.

"That's really sad," I said. And it was. I hadn't really thought about it before but I suppose it was obvious that a reindeer's workload was so strenuous that it could only prove fatal.

"I found out that Santa Claus needs to replace his reindeer every year," he said. "He needs the fittest youngsters he can find – only the healthiest will make it through Christmas Eve, but even the strongest cannot live past Christmas Day. The toll on their bodies... it's too much."

"I'll bet that ruined Christmas for you," I said.

"And you'd be right. But it's not the worst thing."

"There's something worse?"

"What do you think happens to them?" he asked.

"The reindeer? I don't know. Do they get buried?"

"No. They get ground up and used for food."

"Really?   Santa's reindeer?   What, like reindeer steaks?"

"Not food for humans. They've used so much muscle power through the night that their flesh is too tough for people. Even if you slow-cooked it for three days it'd still be as tough as old leather. Santa chops them up and-"

"Santa?" I blurted, appalled.

"Oh, yes. Didn't you know Santa is a butcher? In the old days, his suit was white, all white. But, over the years, enough people have seen him after he's butchered the reindeer that he couldn't continue with white and changed his outfit to red. To hide all the bloodstains, see. The last thing he wants is for a child to see him covered in blood – imagine how *that* would ruin a child's Christmas."

I took a big slurp of coffee and wrinkled my face. It suddenly tasted so bitter. This was the most horrible story I'd ever heard. Santa – a butcher! Chopping up his reindeer! It couldn't be true. But something in the old man's eyes told me it was.

"So what does eat the reindeer?"

"Dogs. They get chopped up and then Santa loads them into a mincer and bags everything up for export. It all ends up in dog food."

"So why the glitter?" I asked.

"A mark of respect. Every bit of dog shit out there contains a little bit of Santa's reindeer. Putting a bit of glitter on the turds is my way of thanking them for their sacrifice."

He sat there and stared at me for a while before lifting his mug and drinking the rest of his tea.

"Happy now that you know?" he asked.

"Not really."

"Well, you know what they say about curiosity. Thanks for the tea, son. I'll be seeing you."

I watched as he shuffled out of the café and he gave a final nod as he passed by the window. I sat there for a while, my thoughts in turmoil. What a downer. This was going to upset me for days. I slowly stood and walked towards the door and the girl behind the counter thanked me for my custom.

I gave her a sad smile. She really was beautiful. I suddenly thought of a way to make the world a happier place, for me at least. Without stopping to consider the possibility that she might turn me down, I opened my mouth and asked her if she'd like to go for a drink somewhere, after she'd finished for the day.

"I'm sorry, I have a boyfriend," she said, looking a little sorry for me. I smiled, nodded, and left the café. It took a few minutes to walk to work and, when I arrived, my boss shouted at me that I'd been late one time too many and sacked me on the spot.

What a horrible day. I didn't think it could get any worse but on the long walk home I stepped in a huge pile of dog shit. I looked down at the horrible brown mess covering the sole of my shoe and noticed that there wasn't even any glitter in it.

Other Books by Steve Roach

Short Story Collections
Glittering Treats - Selected Stories
The Hunt and Other Stories
Resonance
Tiny Wonders

Novellas
Ruiner
People of the Sun
Conquistadors

Travel
Cycles, Tents and Two Young Gents
Mountains, Lochs and Lonely Spots
Step It Up!

Non Fiction
An Alternative Playlist
Retro Arcade Classics
Small People, Big World

Illustrated Books For Children
Crackly Bones
The Terrorer

BONUS CONTENT:

Fishes & Engines

Mr X

Taken from the collection

'Resonance'

Fishes & Engines

Jack MacReady was a dour, miserable bastard, come from a long line of dour, miserable bastards. He knew it. Everybody on the island knew it. Even God knew it. Like his father before him, and his father before that, MacReady fished the waters off the northern coastline of the island. He loved being at sea, even when there was a gale blowing and the boat bobbed about like a cork in a maelstrom. The smell of the brine was in his blood. Cut open a MacReady and salt water would spill out.

His battered trawler had spent countless thousands of nights out on the waters, waters sometimes so ferocious that he had wondered many times whether certain stormy nights would be his last. But always he returned. The MacReady's were famous for their hardiness.

He worked alone and preferred it that way, despite the fact that he had to do everything himself. Other people just got in the way. He'd once been persuaded to take on an apprentice, a young island lad fresh out of school, and he'd been useless. Couldn't tie a decent knot, didn't know his aft from his elbow. Jack tolerated him for two days before sending him packing back to his mother, the Post Mistress who'd forced him onto Jack in the first place. Things had been a little awkward since then, and Jack rarely visited the Post Office anymore.

He didn't mind. He was happy with his own company. His tolerance of other people in general was poor – sometimes it would be months between talking to anybody else, although Jack would think that even this length of time was not long enough.

He had no need of friends. He'd once owned a dog, a stupid clod of a beast that used to get seasick and would throw up all over the deck. Jack had simply turned him loose. A week later, he'd seen the remains by the side of the road. He felt no remorse. If the dog didn't even have enough sense to cross a road that had no more than one or two cars a day passing by, it was for the best that it's time on the Earth was brief.

He fished for himself. He rarely needed money, although there was a considerable sum stuffed underneath his mattress. Sometimes, he scooped it all out and counted it, a methodical process that brought joy into his drab life for a few hours. Spending cash brought on a discomfort bordering on physical pain.   If he had to go shopping, he haggled mercilessly with the shopkeepers, and they were always glad to see the back of him.   He was relentless, and drove a hard bargain.

The other island fishing family, the Buchanans, had called it a day just the previous year, and had wound up the business and moved to the mainland.   The last he'd heard, they were thoroughly regretting it, living in a suburb of Dundee, surviving on State handouts.   He was secretly pleased, even though he had time for old Ike Buchanan.   Less competition meant more fish for him.

He ate what he caught and salted or smoked the leftovers.   Sometimes, if he was feeling up to it, he would drive into the village and set up a stall, and sell what was leftover, but he sometimes struggled for enough fish to justify the bother.   Fishing was a hard business, and age wasn't making it any easier.

His house was bare, with just a few bits of furniture and an old tv set in the corner that hadn't been switched on in years, since they'd cut off the electric supply.   He knew that the modern world had moved on, and the set would no longer work as it used to even with power, but he hadn't yet gotten around to throwing it away. During the rare times he'd watched television in the past, he would look at the idiots parading themselves for the purposes of entertainment and snort with disgust.

The house was functional in a primitive way. He burned driftwood, and if he couldn't find any he went cold. He cooked his dinners, usually fish broth, in a big black pot in the hearth. He got all of his water from a well in the back yard. He had no telephone. The house was a weather-beaten, isolated building on the northern tip of a weather-beaten, isolated island, and Jack MacReady was about as far removed from modern society as it was possible to be.

One bitter morning in March, as MacReady was driving the short distance to the sheltered harbour where he kept his trawler, there was a streak of white light in the Heavens and a heavy object fell from the sky and smashed into the bonnet of the car. The noise was horrendous, a crash that must have reverberated around the entire island. MacReady sat in a stunned silence for a few moments, waiting for the smoke to clear. When he was ready, he clambered out of the car and stood with his hands on his hips, surveying the damage. It was catastrophic. Something had punched a great hole through the bonnet and had wrecked the engine.

"Bastard!" he said.

He looked up at the sky, wondering where the falling object might have come from. There was nothing else up there. He surveyed the empty landscape. He doubted anybody else would drive up this way for days. There was only one thing to do, and he started walking back the way he'd come. A mile down the road, he passed his house and kept walking. The town was only three miles away. A brisk pace would see him there within the hour.

At MacDuff Auto Repairs, brothers Andy and Cathal were chatting about which of the island's two pubs they would frequent that evening. It was a conversation they had engaged in many hundreds of times, and the result was always the same. They would go to The Hungry Cow first to check out the talent for Cathal (usually none, new women only came during the meagre tourist season) before heading off to The Swan to get suitably drunk. It was the same routine three times a week, but they never seemed to tire of it. Once upon a time, before Andy had married Louise and they'd had a daughter, it was seven nights a week. Now, all Cathal wanted to do was settle down and start a family, like his brother.

Cathal looked up to see MacReady walking towards the garage.

"Aye, aye," he said to his brother. "You can deal with this old bugger. I'll go make some coffee."

Cathal disappeared and the old man walked straight over to Andy.

"My car's fucked," he snapped. MacReady wasn't known for his convivial banter.

"Is that so?" asked Andy, wiping his hands on a rag and setting it down.

"Can you come and take a look at it? Have you got much on?"

"We're pretty busy," said Andy, a stock response made more out of habit than anything else. Cathal reckoned that you could always add a bit extra to the bill if the customer thought you were doing them a favour by doing their car first.

MacReady peered over his shoulder and looked as though he didn't believe him.

"Okay, okay," sighed Andy. "Where is it?"

"Top of the island."

"Wait here a minute."

Andy went and spoke to his brother and shortly afterwards he was driving MacReady back along the narrow roads towards the northern end of the island. The drive was conducted mostly in silence, the one brief conversation consisting of:

"Have you any idea what's wrong with it?"

"I already told you. It's fucked."

They reached the broken down vehicle and Andy parked up behind it. MacReady watched as Andy bent over the bonnet and took a good look at the damage. Eventually, he stood back and gave his judgement.

"You're right. It's fucked."

"Didn't I tell you?"

"What happened?"

"Something dropped out of the sky and hit the bloody thing."

"What, like a bit of a plane or something?"

MacReady shrugged. Andy reached inside and put the gears into neutral, and then pushed the car forward a length. After pulling on the handbrake, he returned and looked at the ground. MacReady walked over and joined him.

The hole went down for an undeterminable depth. Whatever it was, the falling object had gone straight through the car and carried on through the soil. Andy leaned over and spat down the hole.

"Can you fix up the car?" asked MacReady.

"No. It's ready for the knacker's yard."

"There's no more miles in it, you say?"

"Only if you want to start pushing it everywhere."

"Damn and fuck!"

Andy gave the rest of the car a cursory inspection. It was a creaking old rust-bucket, ready for scrapping. He was amazed the old duffer had kept it running for so long.

"What about getting a new engine?" asked MacReady.

"I can, but wouldn't it be better all round if you just bought a new car?"

"Do you think I'm made of money? Besides, I don't know how many days I've got left on this Earth. If I drop down dead tomorrow, what'll be the point of having a new car?"

"I meant second hand new, not new-new."

"Just talk to me about the engine. Can you get one scrap, still working?"

"I can, but it still won't be cheap."

MacReady grunted, as though the words had stung.

"What sort of money do you reckon you're talking about?" he asked.

"A few hundred, at least. We'll have to get a second-hand engine imported from one of the scrap yards on the mainland."

"Jay-sus." MacReady felt dizzy, and leaned back against the car for support. Andy watched him carefully, wondering if the old fool was going to have a heart attack.

"Are you OK?"

"Just getting my breath, son. You've given me quite a start."

They waited whilst MacReady regained his composure. Every now and then, the old man would glance over at the youngster as though about to speak, but instead he would clear his throat loudly and say nothing. Eventually, though, he did speak.

"What do you think of a trade?" asked MacReady, his eyes narrowed.

"What sort of trade?"

"How about you fix up my car in return for something that wasn't money?"

Andy's face creased with a smile. He'd heard about the old man's legendary bartering skills, and now it was his turn to be subjected to them. It was a rite of passage, something that all of the islanders encountered at one time or another.

"I'm not sure," he said, shaking his head. "Money works well enough for me. I've a family to support, as you well know."

"Aye, and I'll bet you spend a pretty penny every week on your shopping, eh lad? I know how much food costs these days. How about I give you the cream of my catch, every week from here on in? Think of all that lovely fish you could be eating, all for free. You know how good fish is for a growing bairn – all those omega oils and all that. What do you say?"

Andy thought it over. The weekly shop did put a huge dent in his wages, and he did love eating fish. Plus one of the lads working in the scrap yard owed him a favour – he might even be able to get a replacement engine for the cost of a few beers. No need to let this old fool know that. So the trade would be mostly for the labour, a bit of welding and the like.

"Every week?" he asked. "The best of the catch?"

"Every week. Cod, mackerel, plaice. Sea bass when I get it. The biggest and the best. What do you say?"

Andy knew that Cathal would call him an idiot but there was a certain appeal to the trade. It would cut down on the shopping bill and one could never eat enough fresh fish. Especially if it was free. The wife and bairn might not be so keen on fish, but it'll keep me in lunches and supper, he thought.

"Go on then," he said. "But you'll have to pay for the parts – the trade's only for my labour."

"Aye, if you insist. Just one last little thing," added MacReady, his eyes twinkling beneath his bushy white eyebrows. "I'll pay for my MOT's with cash, as usual, but if you could keep your eye on the old beast and fix up anything minor for free, that'd seal the deal."

"Bloody hell. All right."

MacReady smiled. That was what he was really after – a deal to lock the little bastard into keeping the car in shape forever. He held out his hand and they shook.

A week later, MacReady was back on the road, the replacement engine purring away under the bonnet like a contented panther. After two days at sea, he returned with a decent load, and before he did anything else, he sorted out a plastic crate full of the best fish and packed it with ice. He drove down to MacDuff autos and handed the crate over to Andy, who looked ecstatic with the bounty.

Week in, week out, MacReady returned from the sea and sorted out the best of the catch and packed it into a crate for Andy, who accepted it gratefully. It was a very pleasant deal for everyone. If the trip had been a good one, MacReady would take a second crate to the market and sell from his stall, and any money he made would be added to the pile beneath his mattress. Less money than usual, which he didn't appreciate, but when he thought that his car problems were now effectively over, he felt a little better.

This continued for months.

The car had been in tip-top shape – as much as an old banger like that could be – ever since Andy had repaired it. Nothing else had gone wrong, and MacReady began to feel a bit short-changed, as though Andy hadn't done anything additional within the terms of their agreement.

One day, in a fit of miserableness that was low even for MacReady, he sat down at his kitchen table and worked out how much giving away all of this fish was costing him. With a pencil and a scrap of paper, he worked out how much he could have sold the fish that had so far been given to Andy for free. Nigh on five hundred pounds at top prices, perhaps enough to have paid for the car repairs and be left with no obligation at the end of it.

From that point on, every time MacReady drove down to MacDuff Auto Repairs with a crate full of fish, he felt anger welling up inside him, strong enough to give him an attack of bile. Each week, it got a little bit worse. Andy would accept the fish, seemingly oblivious to the old man's distress, and MacReady would drive home, cursing all the way.

Another two months passed by. After one particularly rough trip at sea, MacReady sat at his kitchen table, fuming, devastated that he'd have to keep on handing over fish to the manky little bastard of a mechanic. He knew he'd made a huge mistake in trying to save a few pounds. He wanted to cancel their agreement, but couldn't see any way out of it without the whole island eventually finding out that he'd broken his word.

Instead, he took the best of the catch to market and sold it off. Afterwards, he drove down to MacDuff Auto Repairs and handed Andy whatever was unsold. A couple of undersized cod, some rockling, goby and the odd weever – an ugly fish that didn't taste particularly nice and needed more work to make into an enjoyable meal.

"There's not so much of the good stuff around at the moment," MacReady explained. "Those bloody Norweigans are taking it all."

Week in, week out this continued. As the days grew a little hotter, by the time the market was over the unsold fish was starting to get a little smelly, the ice having melted hours before. MacReady would begrudgingly spend a pound at the local supermarket for a bag of ice to scatter across the top but it did little to mask the smell.

Once, Andy made a comment about it.

"It's just the crate," snapped MacReady. "I'll give it a swill, if you like."

Each time he saw him, Andy looked a little bit the worse for wear. As though a cumulative effect of eating slightly off fish was having a detrimental effect on his health. About six or seven months after the agreement had started, MacReady delivered his crate to find Cathal talking with Andy's wife. MacReady observed them for a few moments. They looked awfully comfortable with each other.

"Is Andy here?" he asked, interrupting them

Cathal coughed, clearing his throat. He looked as guilty as Judas.

"No," he said, "he's ill."

"Anything serious?"

"Scombroid poisoning, with a dose of salmonella thrown in for good measure. It better not be your bloody fish!"

"How fucking DARE you!" snapped MacReady, feigning outrage.

"I'm sorry," said Cathal, immediately backing down. MacReady slammed the crate down onto the floor and stormed out of the garage.

A week later, whilst drinking in The Swan, he heard the news that Andy was dead. Weakened by the scombroid, the Salmonella had unexpectedly finished him off.

The funeral was on a Friday, and most of the islanders attended, including MacReady. The church was full, and afterwards a large contingent of mourners made their way into the graveyard and watched in silence as the coffin was lowered into a hole in the ground. His young widow stood weeping, holding their baby girl. Cathal stood next to them, his arm around the widow in a comforting gesture. He threw an odd, occasional glance at MacReady, partly accusing and partly, MacReady thought, grateful.

It looked like Cathal, the lonely brother MacDuff, had inherited an instant family.

After the funeral was over, MacReady walked down the narrow road a little while, to where he'd parked his car, half on and half off the verge. Clambering inside, he started the engine and gently lowered the vehicle fully onto the tarmac. At the bottom of the hill, where a T-junction sent the road west towards MacReady's house, and east towards the town, MacReady touched his brakes to bring the car to a halt and found that nothing happened. Further pressure on the brake pedal had no effect. The car continued straight across the junction and ploughed into a low wall on the opposite side.

Shaken, he clambered out of the car and surveyed the damage. The bonnet was badly crumpled, and it looked like the front axle had snapped.

MacReady stood there with his hands on his hips. Nobody else was around. The bleak, empty landscape stretched off in all directions.

It started to rain.

"Bastard!" said MacReady.

He started the long walk home.

Mr X

It came to be known as the Christmas Day Slaughter. A family of four, stabbed with the knife they were using to carve up the turkey. A stack of newly opened presents strewn around the lounge, covered in blood. The furniture, the walls, even the ceiling – all streaked with crimson. A front door kicked in, signs of a forced entry. A mother and her two little girls, murdered.

The father, the husband… the only survivor.

Emerging from a coma after three months, the father is questioned by police. The incident, faded in the minds of newspaper readers, gets fresh life and hits the headlines again. The Christmas Day Slaughter. Can he remember anything? Does he have any idea why a stranger would want to murder his family?

He remembers nothing. Not the days preceding the incident, not the horror of the attack. When the police tell him the details, trying to force the memories to return, he learns again of their terrible injuries. He breaks down, and the doctors ask the police to leave. Come back when he's feeling better, they say.

He never will feel better, but they'll come back anyway.

Fripp enters the nondescript building and climbs the steep staircase. At the top is a door, inset with a small window, and a button. He presses the button and waits. Presently, a serious face peers through the window and looks him over. Fripp holds up a small blue card. The door is opened.

He enters the Pandemonium Club.

Inside, no expense has been spared with the fixtures and fittings. Every inch reeks of opulence, from the crystal chandeliers to the hardwood lining the walls. It is a gentlemen's club, and no women are allowed to pass through the door. Men wander around, dressed in black suits, holding wine glasses and talking quietly amongst themselves.

He walks around, searching the rooms until he finds what he's looking for. Alone, a man sits at a table by the window, reading a battered, antique book. He recognises the man from his picture in the newspapers.

"Professor Cardew?" he asks.

The other man looks up and nods.

"James Fripp," he says, stepping forward.

"Can I help you?"

"I very much hope so. I would like to offer you a proposition."

Cardew looks him over. He closes the book and places it to one side. He beckons him to sit.

"Go on," says Cardew.

"I have money," says Fripp. "As much as it takes."

"I don't doubt that, if they let you join the club," says Cardew, a flicker of disgust on his face.

"It's not as if I can take it with me."

The attempt at humour falls flat. Cardew lets slip a heavy breath of irritation. "What is it that you want?" he asks.

"I want you to build me a time machine."

Cardew stares at him for a few seconds and then hoots with laughter.

"I know you can do it," says Fripp, his voice quiet but bristling with anger. "I've seen what you can do. I read about your wormhole, the thing you put into space. I know about the other professor – Carr, wasn't it? I know how you made him disappear."

"Who told you that?" growls Cardew, his fists clenching.

"There are no secrets here," says Fripp, gesturing towards the rest of the club. "Everybody knows everybody else's business, isn't that right? Isn't that how this all works?"

"So it would seem."

"I have more than enough money to pay you. You can have everything I own, if that's what you require."

Cardew's face turns dark. He sits and studies the man before him. Obviously not an academic but one of the new intake that bought their way in. Standards were slipping. There was a time when you had to be a special sort of person to become a member of the Pandemonium Club, one with the ability to change the world in some way. It was an institution that had survived for hundreds of years, all but unknown to the common man. And now it was going rotten from the inside out by the corrupting force of money. Prime Ministers, men of power, Nobel prize winners and even royalty were the core of the institution, forging a network of links behind the scenes and influencing the way the world went about its business. Now, they were letting in anyone who could buy a membership, regardless of their talents. They were even letting the bloody Freemasons in.

"I'm not interested," says Cardew, returning to his book.

Fripp startles him by taking a firm grip of his arm.

"Hear me out," says Fripp, his eyes flashing with anger. For the first time, Cardew feels like he isn't the one in control of this situation. There's something about Fripp that makes him nervous. The fierceness of his resolve, the hatred and the anger in his voice, and in his eyes.

"Go on," says Cardew.

A man wakes up in a white room, harshly illuminated by spot lights embedded into the walls. He is alone. He is naked. He tries to remember how he got here, what events led to this place. He remembers nothing, not even his own name. He is a blank canvas, a man with no history.

He stands and looks for an exit.

A voice disturbs him, seeming to come from everywhere at once. The room is filled with it.

"Your family has been murdered," says the voice. He can feel it reverberating in his bones.

"You have no one left. Your life has been destroyed. I am the only one that can help you now."

"Who are you?" shouts the man. "Where am I?"

A wall fills with the projected image of a well dressed figure.

"This is the man who killed your family," continues the voice. "I can help you find him. I can give you the tools to take your revenge."

A section of a different wall falls outwards to form a shelf. On it are a bundle of clothes. The man walks across and examines them. Underwear, black trousers and a black shirt. Cold, shivering, he quickly dresses himself. There is a long black coat. A fedora hat. A pair of sunglasses. He dresses and puts on the sunglasses, finding some relief from the harsh lighting. There is a gun, with a photograph next to it. The same photograph that is projected onto the wall. He picks both items up.

"Find him," says the voice. "Find him and kill him."

The lights are extinguished and he stands in a room that is perfectly dark. Thin strands of blue lightning creep up the walls, filling the air with a sizzling sound. A deep thrumming noise begins to shake the floor. I remember this, thinks the man. This has happened before. He screams as the blue lightning flickers out from the walls and wraps itself around his body. He quickly becomes surrounded by it, enveloped by it. The noise and the lightning build to a crescendo and at the end of it, the man is no longer there.

The room is empty once more.

"He must remember nothing of his former life," says Fripp. "Only the search is important now. He must live from moment to moment, his only focus on finding the person in the photograph. Can you make that possible?"

"Anything is possible," says the Hypnotist.

"He must only remember everything when certain words have been spoken. And then I want all of it to come back."

"Just like you said. You're certain you have the right man?"

"I know it's him," says Fripp, his brow creasing with anger.

"This would be a horrendous thing for someone to go through if they were innocent."

"It must be a living nightmare. For what he's taken…. It's the only punishment."

"Wouldn't it just be easier to kill him?"

"No, he must suffer something worse than death."

"This will do it," says the Hypnotist, smiling.

"And you will need to record something I can replay, every time he remembers. When he returns. I'll need to reset his mind. Before it begins again."

"I can do that. It's not a problem."

The man in the fedora hat looks around. He is standing in a strange street, unknown to him. He has no recollection of arriving there. He looks down at himself, at the clothes he wears. The long black coat, the black trousers. These are not his normal clothes, but he doesn't know why he knows this. He can feel the hat on his head, and lifts it off to inspect it. He searches the coat pockets, deep enough to plunge his hands in above the wrists. He pulls out a gun and quickly replaces it.

He pulls out a photograph.

Now he remembers, if only a little. This is the man who murdered my family, he thinks. I will find him and I will kill him.

He starts walking. The streets are empty. A chorus of young voices are shouting from behind a fence and he follows it to the entrance of a school. Children are playing a football match and their parents stand around the touchlines.

He walks over and holds up the photograph to the first adult he comes to.

"Excuse me," he says. "Do you recognise the man in this picture?"

"I will help you," says Cardew. "But it won't be cheap. And there's one obvious question I need you to answer."

"Which is?"

"Why hasn't be been arrested? After everything you told me – the violence, the abuse – surely he's the prime suspect? We can't go near him if the authorities are interested in him. For all I know, he could be under surveillance."

Fripp shakes his head.

"Caroline never reported any of it. I kept asking her to, but she wouldn't listen. There is no official record of abuse."

"You didn't mention it yourself?"

"I thought about it. When they spoke to me, I almost came out with it. It would have been my word against his, of course, and there was no way of knowing they'd believe me. Even if they did, and he was found guilty, he would've been sent to prison and lived a comfortable existence for the next however-many-years until they let him back out again."

"You don't have much confidence in the judicial system?"

Fripp laughs, bitterly. "Does anyone? These people are incarcerated but they only lose their freedom of movement. They can still find some enjoyment in their existence. The prisons no longer seem to operate under a punishment culture, more a rehabilitative one. I don't want to see the bastard rehabilitated – I want him punished. I decided to deal with him myself, once the police had stopped sniffing around."

Cardew thinks for a moment.

"So they think he's a victim," he says.

"Last time I spoke to the police, they told me they were looking for an intruder."

"But you say he ended the episode by stabbing himself?"

"Yes. What of it?"

"There are ways of revealing this – the angle of blade penetration and so on."

"If he had died, and they did an autopsy, then maybe. I don't know."

"Maybe," says Cardew, thinking it over. Fripp waits, inhaling the scents of the club – stale tobacco mixed with furniture polish, and a hint of citrus coming from the short glass vases of pot-pourri scattered around. Eventually, Cardew speaks again.

"Very well. But we will need help."

Fripp leans back in his chair and feels his body relax. Giving his account to Cardew was more exhausting than he'd anticipated. The feelings are still raw. His eyes are glazed with tears.

"What sort of help?" he asks.

"Mind control. For your plan to succeed, and keep succeeding, the subject will have to be programmed before the first event."

"And you know somebody that can do it?"

"He's a member of this club. One that has real power. His company creates software that plugs into corporate systems and distributes mind control messages through audio channels. He's moving into television and film. Pretty soon, we'll have a world filled with mindless automatons, doing the bidding of a few."

"And he will help with this?"

"I think so. If I ask him."

"I don't know how to thank you."

"You don't have to thank me. You just have to pay me."

Langton Matravers finishes his coffee and slams the empty mug down onto the kitchen worktop. He can feel his temper getting out of control again, feel the blood beginning to boil in his veins. He storms out into the hallway and shouts up the stairs.

"Will you get a move on? I'm going to be late!"

Caroline appears at the top of the stairs, looking harassed.

"Effie's just brushing her teeth."

"And Dawn?" he snaps.

"Putting on her uniform."

"Well, just hurry them up."

She disappears and he returns to the kitchen to wait. He forces himself to take a few deep breaths. Now would not be a good time to lose his temper. The last time, so Caroline had told him, he had punched her so hard he'd knocked one of her teeth out. He remembered nothing. Every time he lost control, a new gap appeared in his memory. He needed help, he knew that.

The children hurry down the stairs and wait by the front door. They throw furtive glances at him, as though afraid. Caroline joins them and tries her best to smile. Even down the length of the hallway, he can see the fear in her eyes. He walks towards them and, as he reaches up for his coat, Caroline flinches.

Fripp listens to his daughter and feels his own rage building. The physical and mental abuse. The way the children are in danger. He feels like driving over to Langton's place of work and dragging him outside to administer a beating so severe he'd never lay a finger on his family ever again. But Fripp is too old for that kind of thing. A few years ago, maybe.

"It's not safe for you to stay," he says. "Or the children."

"He's promised never to hurt us again."

"And how many times have we heard that?"

"Dad, please. You're not helping."

"What do you want me to say? Do you want me to pretend that everything's normal? To just accept that my daughter and my grandchildren are victims of domestic abuse and carry on and smile as though nothing's happening?"

Caroline wipes tears away from her eyes and stares at the floor for a few moments.

"I don't know…." she says in a quiet voice.

"He'll keep doing it," says Fripp, unable to hide the anger in his voice. "And it'll get worse. And then, one day, he'll end up killing you."

"Stop being so dramatic, Dad."

"Listen to yourself. It's like you're in some sort of denial."

"I love him! He wasn't always like this. You should see him after he calms down… he cries like a baby and promises he'll never do it again. I believe him."

"Carrie….."

"We'll get back to normal, you'll see."

The white van pulls up outside the Fripp residence and two men clamber out. After getting their toolbags from the back, they ring the doorbell and wait. Presently, the door is opened by a man in a beige leisure suit.

"Morning Mr Fripp!" they chime.

"Good morning," he says, stepping aside to let them in. They are led through a hallway, past the lounge and dining room, and into the kitchen. A new annexe is nearing completion at the far end of the house. They walk inside and look around.

"Should be just another day or two now," says Charlie.

"Just the finishing touches," says Dave, nodding.

"Excellent," says Fripp, smiling.

They are interrupted by the loud ringtone of Charlie's mobile phone. Notes from Grieg's 'In the Hall of the Mountain King' bounce around the freshly plastered walls of the extension. There are gaps in the plaster, waiting for some kinds of fitting. There are no windows. In the corner are a couple of tins of white paint and some sealed boxes. Charlie excuses himself for a moment and answers the call.

"Hello Mr Knapp," he says brightly. He listens for a few moments before speaking again. "Not a problem. Yes, hopefully tomorrow afternoon, the day after at the latest. OK then. Bye."

Fripp looks over with a curious expression on his face.

"Was that John Knapp?" he asks.

"It was, yeah. Got a leak in his swimming pool. You know him, then?"

"We're members of the same club," says Fripp.

"Golf?" asks Dave.

"More of a gentlemen's club."

"Say no more," says Dave, doing a passable Eric Idle impersonation.

"So," says Charlie, putting his phone away, "you want the lights and speakers fitting, then a kind of ledge-stroke-table in the wall here?"

"Yes."

"The projector goes up top and then we'll fit and cover those circuit board things before everything gets painted white – is that right?"

"That's correct," says Fripp. "And the circuit wires come through to the kitchen."

"Are we fitting something on the other end?"

"No, I have a friend who will attend to that."

"Fair enough."

"And remember not to put any handles or markers on the inside of the door. I want the walls to blend."

"Not a problem," says Charlie.

"Well, I'll leave you to it," says Fripp.

After he's gone, Charlie looks at Dave and smiles.

"Miserable old bugger could offer to make us a cuppa. I could murder a coffee."

"Whose turn is it to walk to Costa Coffee?"

"Mine. Do you want to get started on fitting the lights? I'll be back in twenty minutes."

Before he leaves, Charlie takes out his wallet and checks the contents.

"Spot me a tenner, will you Dave? Looks like the missus has rifled my cash."

"No worries."

Dave pulls out his wallet and opens it. A piece of paper flutters out and drifts across the room to land at Charlie's feet. He picks it up and gives it a cursory inspection.

"A Holiday Inn receipt, Dave?"

Dave coughs and looks a little embarrassed.

"Hand it over, Charlie."

"You been arguing with the missus again?"

"Something like that."

"This is for last Tuesday. You could have stayed over at mine. The missus was out for the night at an old college friend's, playing bridge or whatever it is that they get up to. We could've had a few beers."

"Thanks, Charlie. It's all good now though."

Charlie hands over the slip of paper and smiles. He walks around to the garden gate, heading for the nearby shopping precinct. Dave watches him go and then crumples the receipt before stuffing it into his pocket. That was a close one, he thinks. One day, he'll put two and two together.

Fripp sits in his kitchen, a half full tumbler of whisky on the counter in front of him. Next to it is a small electronic Dictaphone. He takes a sip of the whisky and clears his throat. Reaching down, he picks up the Dictaphone and presses the record button.

"Your family has been murdered," he says. "You have no one left. Your life has been destroyed. I am the only one that can help you now."

He presses the button again, halting the recording. He should have let the Hypnotist take care of this aspect of the plan. Matravers was going to recognise his voice and he'd begin to understand what was happening to him. Fripp finishes off the drink and deletes the recording before starting again, this time in a deeper voice.

"Your family has been murdered. You have no one left. Your life has been destroyed. I am the only one that can help you now." He pauses for a moment before continuing. "This is the man who killed your family. I can help you find him. I can give you the tools to take your revenge."

He presses the button and flicks through the menu to replay this latest attempt. He listens as the cold words echo around the kitchen.

"Do you recognise the man in this picture?"

The woman studies the photograph for a moment before handing it back.

"I'm sorry," she says, "I don't." She picks up her shopping bags and walks away. The figure in the black coat watches her go. He feels his shoulders slump in despair. She was the fiftieth person he'd asked, just another in a long line of people who are unable to help.

He couldn't give up. The need to find the man in the photograph is all he can think about. Every moment is consumed by the desire to hunt him down. He looks around at the interior of the mall, a huge complex swarming with people. One of them must know who is in the picture.

He approaches a short, stocky woman and holds up the photo.

"Do you recognise the man in this picture?" he asks.

The woman leans forward for a better look and squints. After a moment, she leans back and looks at him.

"Can you take off your hat?" she asks.

"My hat?"

"Yeah. Let me get a better look at you."

He obliges and waits.

"It's you," she says.

At the sound of those words, images fire up in front of his vision, projected somehow onto the inside of the lenses of his sunglasses. He sees his dead wife lying on the floor in a pool of blood, her body ravaged by stab wounds. The image is replaced with another, this time of his daughter Effie, her throat slit. She's still wearing a paper crown from a Christmas cracker, the gold foil splattered with her blood. There's a picture of Dawn, his little angel. What he sees makes him shake with a sudden sob of anguish. The pictures are replaced by others, all equally as grisly.

And he remembers.

He remembers killing his family, hacking them to pieces with a large knife. He remembers coming to his senses and realising what he'd done. Searching for a way to undo the carnage. He remembers opening the front door and closing it behind himself before turning around and kicking it through in the hope that it will look like an intruder has forced his way in.

Finally, he remembers plunging the knife into himself, over and over before collapsing.

So he was the murderer. All of this time spent searching for himself. He remembers the gun in his coat pocket and pulls it out. As the woman before him screams in horror, he raises it to his temple and pulls the trigger.

The world is instantly consumed by darkness.

As he exits the house, closing the new front door behind himself, he's approached by two men in dark clothing. They are both wearing beeny hats and look like hired muscle.

"Langton Matravers?" asks one.

"Who's asking?" he says, and before he knows what's happening the man who asked his name throws a punch and sends him reeling. A follow-up punch renders him senseless. Unconscious, he's picked up by the men and carried to a battered, pale yellow transit van. They open the rear doors and throw him inside. One climbs in after him and closes the door. He secures Matravers' wrists and ankles with cable ties, and tears off a strip of duct tape to cover his mouth.

Shortly after, the van pulls up alongside the Fripp house. After a brief check to see nobody is looking, they drag the still unconscious Matravers from the van and carry him through to the new extension. They lay him on the floor and leave.

Fripp is waiting, along with Cardew and the Hypnotist.

"This is ground zero," says Cardew. "Where it all begins."

A muddy field is being used as a car park. Half of it has been covered with tarmac, and the unfinished work looks a mess. To the side, a hot dog stand squats, taped off and out of business. The man in the black coat and fedora hat walks up to people, holding up a photograph. Nobody can help. He feels his shoulders slump with despair.

He comes to a young man and asks the question. Always the same question.

"It's you," says the young man. "Even without the hat and glasses, I can tell it's you."

Moments later, the man in the black coat and fedora hat produces a gun, raises it to his temple and pulls the trigger.

"So it's a real gun?" asks Fripp, turning the revolver over in his hands.

"It is," says Cardew, nodding. "With a single bullet. Once he hears the trigger phrase, he'll only need the one."

"And you say it's actually a part of the time machine?"

Cardew nods again.

"This gun is more than just a way of firing a bullet – once it's fired, as well as doing the obvious, it also remotely initiates the recall system back in the charge room. It's all connected – the gun, the hat, the coat, the sunglasses – it's all a way of getting him to carry around this part of the machine without him knowing it."

"I see," says Fripp. "So blowing his brains out can be undone, every time?"

"Of course. The whole thing would be pointless if he could only kill himself once. The firing of the gun is the end of the loop. At the beginning of the loop, he will be intact."

"Back at the charge room?"

"Yes. He won't know it but there will be circuitry sewn into the clothing. The hat will act as a GPS, so he can be constantly tracked until the moment the gun is fired and he's brought back to your house. The sunglasses will, upon hearing the trigger phrase, bombard him with images from the crime scene and bring back his memories. The memories lead to the gun. The coat contains components that are integral to the operation of the machine. Everything is tied together."

"And when he's blown his brains out? The machine puts him back together again, is that right?"

"Strictly speaking, it's not a time machine," explains Cardew, using the tone of voice he usually reserves for his slower university students. "The equipment will generate a variable time loop, a closed circuit that repeats once the gun has been fired. Wherever he is, he'll be brought back to this room intact, ready for the priming sequence to begin again. This will go on forever, or until you think he's had enough."

"Forever isn't long enough."

"That's your prerogative. How are you going to get him to come here, initially?"

"I know a couple of bruisers that will help me out," says Fripp.

"I'll make sure the Hypnotist is with us. How long before you're ready?"

"I have a couple of builders coming to finish off the charge room tomorrow."

"Have they any idea what they're putting together?"

"They think it's a cinema room."

Cardew smiles.

"Let me know when they're finished. I have the control panel, so once they're done I can wire that up to the system and we should be ready to begin."

It is Fripp's turn to smile. He can't wait to get started.

Caroline Matravers carries the turkey through to the lounge and places the tray onto a raised metal grille. Langton sits in silence, watching her. She sits at the end of the table, opposite her husband, the children on either side. Around the room, opened presents lie stacked up in little piles. The girls, innocent to the tension between their parents, have had a wonderful morning, rising early and pulling their mother out of bed to come downstairs and open their presents.

Langton had remained in bed, listening to their laughter, angry that they were keeping him awake. It wasn't even seven o'clock before the girls rushed in and woke them up. At eight, unable to get back to sleep, he'd got out of bed and dressed. He went downstairs, straight to the kitchen, and opened a bottle of wine. He downed a large glass before refilling it.

Six hours later, as he sat before the feast Caroline had patiently spent the rest of the morning preparing, his head was pounding and he struggled to contain his anger. All this noise! Children squealing, cutlery clanking, the television blaring away in the corner of the room. Everybody moving, nobody staying still, not even for a minute.

"Shall I carve the turkey?" asks Caroline.

"What?" he says, irritated beyond belief. All he wants to do is go somewhere and lie down. Somewhere far away, where there are no children, no bitch of a wife to keep nagging him. Somewhere where the endless bills can't reach him, where he can escape the relentless pressure, the endless grind of crawling through each new day his world brings. How did his life turn out this way? Bogged down with a family of cretins, swamped with debt, living a life he loathed? His head swam, anger pulsing in black waves, his skull feeling like it was about to explode.

"Langton? Shall I carve the turkey?" asks his wife in a nervous voice.

He looks at her. He reaches out for the carving knife. He stands there, gently swaying for a moment, trying to clear his mind.

Do it! says a voice inside his head. Kill them.

His grip tightens on the handle of the knife.

He wakes up naked, in a room he doesn't recognise. His head pounds and he reaches up to dab at a tender spot around his jaw. The pain makes him wince.

"Hello, Langton," says a voice.

He turns around and sees a man sitting on a stool, watching him.

"What is this?" asks Langton, standing up. "Where am I?"

"You are at the dawn of a new life," says the man.

Langton looks around the room, searching for a way out. There doesn't appear to be a door. The room is white, with no furniture apart from the stool.

"What the fuck is going on?" he asks.

"Relax, Langton," says the man with the soothing voice. Just hearing him speak those two words makes some of the tension leave his body.

"What do you want?"

"I want you to empty your mind of all thought."

"Why? Let me out of here. I don't know what this is but I'm warning you-"

"Please, Langton. Relax. Take a few deep breaths. Once you listen to what I have to say, you can go."

Langton feels himself relax. There is something about the man's voice that makes him want to listen. Something about his eyes that demands a calm silence.

"I want you to listen to my voice," says the man. "Nothing else matters. There is only my voice. Empty your mind of all thought."

On the other side of one of the walls, Fripp and Cardew stand in the kitchen, watching the Hypnotist go about his work on a small monitor. The sound has been muted. The Hypnotist warned that they shouldn't listen, in case they inadvertently start following the suggestions being made to Matravers.

Fifteen minutes pass, in which Fripp makes them both a cup of coffee and smokes a cigarette. During this time, they see Matravers become more and more relaxed, totally under the power and influence of the Hypnotist. Fripp knows roughly what is being said in that room.

Matravers' mind is being wiped, cleared of all memories except for one – the day he killed his family.   When the Hypnotist has finished, Matravers won't remember anything except the brutal murders, but even this will be buried.

Even this will only be recalled when Matravers hears the trigger phrase.

It's you.

He won't remember anything else from his personal history, or even his own name.

Langton Matravers will be a blank canvas.

Unknown to himself.

Mr X.

The   Hypnotist   will   then   begin   the programming.   He will instil an all-consuming urge to find a mystery man, the one who killed his family. Nothing else will matter. Only the search.   And   once   the   programming   is complete, the Hypnotist will tell Matravers to fall asleep, and to wake only at the sound of the single toll of a bell.

When it's over, Matravers is lying on the floor, asleep. Fripp opens the door and they return to the   kitchen.   He   nods   at   Cardew,   who immediately begins pressing buttons on a small wall panel. A minute later, Cardew looks at Fripp.

"The loop is now open," he says. "Turn up the volume and listen."

They stand in silence. From the room next door comes the automated sound of a bell tolling. On the small monitor, they see Langton Matravers wake up and look around, wondering where he is. A recording of Fripp's voice begins.

"Your family has been murdered....."

It could be anywhere in the country, the starting co-ordinates are random. But they can be over-ridden. Sometimes, Fripp manually sets the co-ordinates and heads out in his car to meet him.

It's the same every time.

Fripp walks around until he spots the man in the fedora hat. The long black coat. The sunglasses. He watches him for a while, holding up a photograph to strangers, asking them the same question, over and over.

And, every time Fripp walks over, the man spots him and approaches.

Fripp cannot see the man's eyes behind the sunglasses, but he can hear the desperation in his voice. The need to find the man in the photograph is apparent in every tired gesture. Sometimes, Matravers can go for more than a week before someone sees the photograph for what it is.

"Do you recognise the man in this picture?" asks the man in black.

Fripp pauses, preparing himself to savour what comes next.

"It's you," he says at last.

Printed in Great Britain
by Amazon